MIKE
THE KNIGHT™

Meet Mike!

by HIT Entertainment

Simon Spotlight

SIMON SPOTLIGHT

An imprint of Simon & Schuster Children's Publishing Division
1230 Avenue of the Americas, New York, New York 10020
© 2013 Hit (MTK) Limited. Mike the Knight™ and logo and
Be a Knight, Do It Right!™ are trademarks of Hit (MTK) Limited.
Nickelodeon and all related titles and logos are trademarks of
Viacom International Inc. All rights reserved, including the right of
reproduction in whole or in part in any form. SIMON SPOTLIGHT
and colophon are registered trademarks of Simon & Schuster, Inc.
For information about special discounts for bulk purchases,
please contact Simon & Schuster Special Sales at 1-866-506-1949
or business@simonandschuster.com.
Manufactured in the United States of America   1012 LAK
First Edition 10 9 8 7 6 5 4 3 2 1
ISBN 978-1-4424-7429-1
ISBN 978-1-4424-7430-7 (eBook)

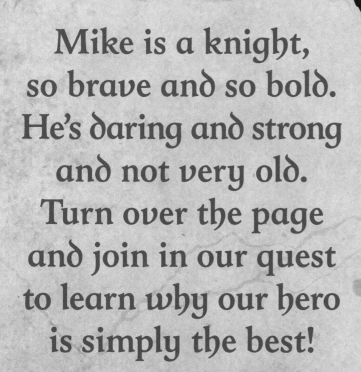

Mike is a knight,
so brave and so bold.
He's daring and strong
and not very old.
Turn over the page
and join in our quest
to learn why our hero
is simply the best!

I'm Mike the Knight.
Welcome to Glendragon! I'm a
knight-in-training. My mission
is to be a brave hero, just like
my dad, the King.

If you need to defend a castle or round up Vikings, I'm at your service! Knights always try to do the right thing. If I get stuck, I open my *Big Book for Little Knights-in-Training*.

I spend most days in Glendragon Castle practicing my knightly skills . . . but if someone needs help, I can be dressed in my armor faster than you can say "Huzzah!"

After I put on my armor, I grab my sword and shield. Knights never leave their castles without them. We always need to be ready for an adventure!

Then I saddle up Galahad, my trusty horse! He's the
finest horse in Glendragon. He is an expert at trotting and
galloping . . . and can even tiptoe when we need to be quiet.

Galahad is also my friend, and I take good care of
him. Whenever he needs new horseshoes, I take him to
Mr. Blacksmith's stall. Whenever he gallops through mud puddles,
I take him to Hairy Harry's Horse Wash for a good scrub.

Now I'm honored to introduce my two best friends, who are both dragons! Sparkie is a gigantic dragon who breathes fire . . . and is the castle cook! Squirt is a little dragon with a very big heart. He can't breathe fire like Sparkie, but he is an expert at squirting water!

Sparkie and Squirt are the best, bravest friends around. If one of us gets into trouble, the others always come to the rescue!

This is my little sister, Evie. She's a wizard-in-training, but she still has a lot to learn. Her magic spells never seem to work out quite right. Once, by mistake, she shrank me, Sparkie, and Squirt to the size of mice!

Even though she's still learning magic, Evie and I make a great team! When our mom, Queen Martha, is impressed with our teamwork, she gives us royal prizes, like these scarves! Thanks, Mom!

My mom asks me to lend a knightly hand and help protect the kingdom when my dad, the King of Glendragon, is away. He often travels to faraway lands—rescuing villages, battling sea monsters, and discovering new castles—but he sends lots of postcards telling us all about his amazing adventures.

While some missions call for great courage, a knight's work isn't always exciting. We also have to do chores like helping to clean up the castle. Evie wishes she could use magic to do her chores, but there's no magic allowed!

My missions have led me to the
farthest corners of Glendragon! I've
searched beaches for treasure, followed
trails into the Tall Tree Woods, and
climbed grassy mountains.

I've even discovered a ship of rowdy Vikings—and lived to tell the tale.

I'm Mike the Knight! I'm not afraid of anything!

Sometimes my missions lead me to new friends. The first time I explored the Maze Caves, I met a family of trolls.

Now whenever I visit, Ma Troll bakes a special treat for me, and Pa Troll sings, dances, and gives me friendly pats on the back.

I'm also friends with Ma and Pa Troll's son, Trollee. He wants to be a knight, just like me! We do all kinds of things together from treasure hunts to knightly games.

When I'm not on a quest, you can find me back home
at Glendragon Castle. It has everything a knight needs: a
ball for feasts, a throne room, and a real jousting arena!

Galahad and I spend lots of time training in the arena!
We practice jousting with a lance and riding through
obstacle courses. When it's time for a jousting match, the
whole kingdom comes to watch! If we try our hardest,
Galahad and I sometimes win a trophy!

Even if I don't win a trophy, I never give up. It's the first
rule of being a knight! When times are tough, I know that
Glendragon is full of friends to help make things right again.

So what will my next adventure be? We'll have to wait and see, but if someone needs my help, you can count on me to rush to the rescue! By my sword, I'm Mike the Knight!

Thanks for visiting Glendragon
with me. As I always say,
**"Be a knight,
do it right!"**